Walt Disney

Snow White and the Seven Dwarfs

Twin Books

Once upon a time, in a faraway castle, there lived a lovely little Princess named Snow White. Her vain and wicked stepmother, the Queen, feared that someday Snow White's beauty would surpass her own. So she dressed the little Princess in rags and forced her to work very hard. Snow White obeyed the Queen without complaint.

Each day the vain Queen consulted her magic mirror. "Magic mirror on the wall, who is the fairest one of all?"

"You, O Queen, are the fairest in the land," the mirror would reply.

Then the Queen would smile with pleasure. However, Snow White was growing up, and ragged clothes could not hide her beauty.

Snow White did not know of her stepmother's jealousy. She did her work with a smile, all the while daydreaming of a handsome Prince who might find her and carry her away to his castle. One morning, as she drew water from a well, she made a wish that someday her dream would come true.

Much to her surprise, after Snow White made her wish, a handsome young Prince appeared. He was taken by her beauty. Snow White fled to the tower balcony where she gazed shyly down at her Prince. As he sang of love, Snow White placed a kiss upon her friend the dove, who took it to the Prince. Then Snow White disappeared behind a curtain in the tower.

The wicked Queen had witnessed the meeting between Snow White and the Prince. She was now even more envious of Snow White's beauty. She summoned the huntsman.

"Take Snow White far into the forest," she said. "There you will kill her. Bring back her heart in this."

The Queen handed the huntsman a golden box. Even though he was unwilling, the huntsman knew he must not fail.

The huntsman took Snow White deep into the forest. Snow White sang joyfully, thinking of nothing but her Prince. She gathered flowers along the way.

Just then, Snow White heard the cry of a baby bird. She knelt to pick it up.

Snow White was kind toward every living thing. "Your mama and papa can't be far," she assured the little bird.

Snow White waved to the little bird as it flew away home. But as she turned to continue her walk, she saw the huntsman with his dagger drawn, ready to strike. She screamed. Then the huntsman fell to his knees. "I can't do it! he cried. "Forgive me."

He told Snow White about the Queen's evil order that he was to kill her and bring back her heart. "She's mad. . .jealous of you. Run away! Hide, and never come back!" he warned. "I shall kill a deer and put its heart in the box."

Snow White was very frightened. She did what the huntsman said and ran deep into the forest.

The forest was very dark. And the farther Snow White ran, the darker it became. An owl hooted and bats flew overhead. Even the trees seemed to grab at Snow White as she ran past. Eyes shone everywhere in the darkness. It was a frightening place.

Faster and faster the Princess ran, until she could run no farther. She fell to the ground and burst into tears. And while she wept, bright eyes peered at her from behind the trees.

Snow White looked up and saw dozens of forest animals all around her. They approached Snow White cautiously, but soon found they had nothing to fear. Snow White told them all about the Queen and the huntsman. Then she dried her eyes and sang a song to her new friends.

"I really feel quite happy now," she said as she walked along with the forest animals. "But I do need a place to sleep at night."

The animals knew just where to take her. The raccoons took hold of her skirt and led her through the forest, while the deer and the rabbits and the squirrels followed happily along.

They stopped at the edge of a clearing. Show White pushed aside the bushes and saw a perfect little cottage among the trees.

"Oh, it's lovely!" she cried.

She ran toward the house, over a little bridge, and up to a window. She peered in, but could see nothing. And since no one seemed to be at home, she went inside.

Inside the cottage Snow White saw seven little chairs.

"It must be seven little children who live here—seven untidy little children!" she remarked to the animals.

As she looked around her, she saw that everything was indeed quite untidy. There were dishes in the sink, dust on the fireplace, and cobwebs everywhere.

"I know. We'll clean the house and surprise them," she said. "Then maybe they'll let me stay."

Together Snow White and the animals cleaned the little cottage until it was very neat and tidy.

When they finished downstairs, Snow White and the animals went upstairs to see what they could find there. At the top of the stairs was a door, and beyond the door Snow White saw seven little beds.

"And look, they have names carved on them," said Snow White, and she read each name aloud. "Doc, Happy, Sneezy, Dopey, Grumpy, Bashful and Sleepy." Then she yawned. "I'm a little sleepy myself," she said. She stretched across three beds and fell fast asleep.

Meanwhile, in a cave nearby, seven little men were busy digging for diamonds. They were the very same dwarfs who lived in the cottage that Snow White had found in the forest. Each day they worked in their diamond mine deep inside the mountain.

Doc stood at a table and peered at the diamonds through a jeweler's glass. The good diamonds were saved, and the bad ones were tossed away. Dopey swept up the bad diamonds. Each dwarf had a special job to do.

It was time to return home. With picks over their shoulders, the Seven Dwarfs marched in a line. Doc was in the lead, followed by Grumpy, Happy, Sleepy, Sneezy and Bashful. Dopey brought up the rear.

As the dwarfs marched home, they sang a happy song. They had worked hard and were tired and hungry.

But when the dwarfs reached the cottage, Doc noticed a light in the house. He stopped in his tracks.

"Look! The lits light, I mean the light's lit! Something's in there!" he cried.

The dwarfs bravely followed Doc to the house to investigate.

The dwarfs opened the door and crept slowly into the house, careful not to make a sound.

"Careful, men," Doc whispered. The others tiptoed into the house behind him.

"Look! The floor's been swept," said Doc.

"Chair's been dusted," said Grumpy.

"Our window's been washed," added Happy.

Bashful looked up at the ceiling. "Gosh," he said. "Our cobwebs are missing."

"The whole place is clean!" said Doc.

"There's dirty work afoot!" Grumpy grumbled. He was suspicious.

The dwarfs all looked at one another. Then they smelled a delicious smell.

"Something's cooking," said Happy.

The dwarfs heard a noise upstairs.

"One of us has got to go down and chase it up. . . I mean. . . go up and chase it down," muttered Doc. The dwarfs quickly elected Dopey to lead the way.

"Don't be afraid. We're right behind you," they all whispered.

Quietly and carefully they climbed the stairs to the bedroom. Then they slowly tiptoed into the room, where they saw a sheeted figure stretched across the beds.

Snow White stretched and yawned under the sheet. The dwarfs were certain it was some kind of monster.

"Let's kill it before it wakes up!" they whispered.

They raised their weapons in the air, ready to strike.

Doc quickly pulled the sheet back.

"Why, it's a girl!" he exclaimed.

Snow White was quite startled to see seven little men peering at her from the foot of the bed.

"Why, you're little men," she said as she sat up. "How do you do?"

The dwarfs were quite relieved that Snow White wasn't a monster.

Snow White could easily guess the name that belonged to each dwarf, especially Grumpy. Snow White folded her arms in an imitation of him. "Oh, you must be Grumpy," she said with a giggle.

Then Snow White introduced herself and told them all about the wicked Queen. "Please don't send me away," she pleaded. "If you do, she'll kill me."

The dwarfs took pity on Snow White. And when she told them that she would clean and cook for them, they quickly decided that she must stay—all except Grumpy. He wanted nothing to do with a wicked Queen, or a Princess.

At the castle, the Queen thought Snow White was dead. She held the box that she thought contained Snow White's heart, and she asked the mirror again, "Magic mirror on the wall, who now is the fairest one of all?"

But the mirror replied, "Over the seven jeweled hills, beyond the seventh fall, in the cottage of the Seven Dwarfs, dwells Snow White, fairest one of all."

The Queen was enraged. Snow White still lived!

Furiously, the Queen descended a winding staircase to a dark dungeon beneath the castle. There was a hidden room filled with bottles, potions and a book of magic spells. She opened the book to a spell for a disguise and mixed a terrible potion. Then she drank it and was transformed into an ugly old hag.

The Queen then found another spell, and following the recipe carefully, filled her cauldron with a bubbling liquid. She took an apple and slowly dipped it into the cauldron.

"And now," she cackled, "a special sort of death for one so fair. One taste of this poisoned apple and the victim's eyes will close forever! Then I shall be fairest of them all!"

At the cottage of the Seven Dwarfs, it was time for dinner.

"You'll just have time to wash," Snow White decided. "Let me see your hands."

One by one, the dwarfs slowly pulled their hands from behind their backs and showed them to Snow White.

"Worse than I thought," she said. "March straight outside and wash, or you'll not get a bite to eat."

All Seven Dwarfs marched outside to wash. They really didn't want to wash, but they were willing to do so for the Princess—all except Grumpy. "Her wiles are beginnin' to work!" he grumbled.

Six dwarfs quickly scrubbed up. Then they all turned to Grumpy. And, before he knew what was happening, they jumped on him!

"Get 'im!" shouted Doc.

They grabbed Grumpy and pulled him over to the tub, where they washed him up. Now all seven were ready for dinner.

After dinner it was time for a party. The dwarfs played their musical instruments while Snow White danced around the room.

Each dwarf took a turn dancing with Snow White. As a special surprise, Dopey climbed onto Sneezy's shoulders. Then he covered them both up with a long cloak. Now he was as tall as Snow White!

Dopey was having a good time until Sneezy sneezed him right off his shoulders! Everyone laughed.

While laughter rang throughout the forest, the wicked Queen prepared for her journey to the home of the Seven Dwarfs. Disguised as a peddler woman, she left the castle by way of the moat that separated the castle from the forest. An evil gleam flashed in her eyes as she rowed toward the forest's edge. A basket of shiny red apples lay at her feet.

The next morning the dwarfs set out for the diamond mine. One by one they said goodbye to Snow White and each received a kiss on his head in return.

Even Grumpy didn't seem to mind being kissed by Snow White. "Now, I'm warning you," he said, "don't let anybody into the house!"

"Why, Grumpy! You do care!" she said.

After she had waved goodbye to the Seven Dwarfs, Snow White decided to make them a pie for dinner. As she rolled out the dough, her animal friends looked on. She especially wanted to make the pie for Grumpy because he seemed to like her after all.

As Snow White worked, she thought about the handsome Prince she had met at the castle. She wished he would find her.

Just then an old woman appeared outside the window. "All alone, my pet?" she asked.

The animals were frightened by the old woman, and they scurried away to hide.

"It's apple pies that make the menfolks' mouths water," said the peddler. She offered Snow White a taste from a juicy red apple she had in her basket.

The animals sensed that something was wrong. The birds flew at the old woman, but Snow White didn't understand what her friends were trying to do. She shooed the birds away and invited the old woman inside. The animals knew they must find the dwarfs and bring them back to help.

They ran and flew as quickly as they could, the birds chirping an alarm. When they finally reached the mine, they found the dwarfs hard at work. They pulled and tugged at the dwarfs' clothing.

"They aren't acting this way for nothing," Grumpy said.

"Maybe the Queen's got Snow White," Sleepy said with a yawn.

The Queen! That was it! There was no time to lose. The dwarfs grabbed their picks and clubs and ran to rescue Snow White.

But they were too late. Snow White had taken a bite of the poisoned apple. As she fell to the floor, the fruit rolled away from her limp hand.

The witch cackled cruelly. "Now, I'll be the fairest in the land!" she gloated. "The only thing that can save her is Love's First Kiss, and there's no chance of that."

Dark clouds were gathering and lightning flashed across the sky. The witch ran out of the cottage into a pouring rain.

The dwarfs arrived just in time to see the wicked Queen disappear into the forest.

"There she goes!" cried Grumpy.

In hot pursuit, they chased her to the base of a rocky cliff. The rain came down so hard they could hardly see. Thunder boomed and lightning flashed.

"After her!" cried Grumpy over the thunder.

The wicked Queen climbed up the cliff and was soon trapped on a narrow ledge. She began to pry loose a large boulder to send it toppling onto the dwarfs below.

"Look out!" cried Grumpy to the others.

The witch cackled triumphantly as the heavy boulder began to move.

Suddenly, a bolt of lightning split the air and hit the ledge upon which the Queen was standing. The ledge broke away from the rocky cliff.

With a deafening shriek, the Queen toppled into the black abyss below, never to be seen again.

When the weary dwarfs returned to the cottage, they found Snow White lying on the floor. Gently, they lifted her up and placed her on her bed. Tears streamed down their faces as they knelt beside their beloved Snow White.

Snow White was so beautiful, even in death, that the dwarfs could not find it in their hearts to bury her. They fashioned a coffin of glass and gold and kept a constant vigil at her side.

BLANCHE-NEIGE

Far away, Snow White's Prince heard of the maiden who slept in the glass coffin. He had searched far and wide to find Snow White. Finally, one day, riding through the trees, he saw her. He dismounted from his horse and went to the coffin. Carefully, he removed the glass lid and gazed upon her beauty once more.

Slowly the Prince knelt down and gently kissed Snow White. Then, with the dwarfs and the animals, he bowed his head in silence.

Suddenly, Snow White began to stir. She sat up and rubbed her eyes.

Snow White was alive!

Joyously, the Prince gathered her in his arms, while shouts of joy rang out around them. The dwarfs hugged each other with delight.

Snow White kissed each dwarf goodbye. Then the Prince lifted her up onto his horse and led her away to his castle on the hill.

And they lived happily ever after.

Produced by
Twin Books,
15 Sherwood Place,
Greenwich, CT 06830

ISBN 1 85469 987 3

Reprinted in 1992

Printed in Hong Kong